Countries of the World

Sweden

by Janet Riehecky

Consultant:
Annette Lernvik-Djupström
The American Swedish Institute

Bridgestone Books
an imprint of Capstone Press
Mankato, Minnesota

Bridgestone Books are published by Capstone Press
151 Good Counsel Drive, P.O. Box 669, Mankato, Minnesota 56002
http://www.capstone-press.com

Library of Congress Cataloging-in-Publication Data
Riehecky, Janet, 1953–
    Sweden/by Janet Riehecky.
    p. cm.—(Countries of the world)
    Includes bibliographical references and index.
    Summary: Discusses the land, people, and culture of Sweden.
    ISBN 0-7368-0629-6
    1. Sweden—Juvenile literature. [1. Sweden.] I. Title. II. Countries of the world
(Mankato, Minn.)
    DL609 .R54 2001
    948.5—dc21   00-024191

Editorial Credits

Tom Adamson, editor; Timothy Halldin, designer; Heidi Schoof and Kimberly Danger,
    photo researchers

Photo Credits

Ingrid Mårn Wood, 8
International Stock/Chad Ehlers, 6, 10, 16, 18
North Wind Picture Archives, 20
Photo Network/Chad Ehlers, cover, 12
StockHaus Limited, 5 (top)
Visuals Unlimited/Ernest Manewal, 5 (bottom); George Herben, 14

1 2 3 4 5 6 06 05 04 03 02 01

Table of Contents

Name: Kingdom of Sweden
Capital: Stockholm
Population: Almost 9 million
Language: Swedish
Religion: Evangelical Lutheran

Size: 173,731 square miles
(449,963 square kilometers)
*Sweden is a little larger than the
U.S. state of California.*
Crops: Grain, sugar beets, potatoes

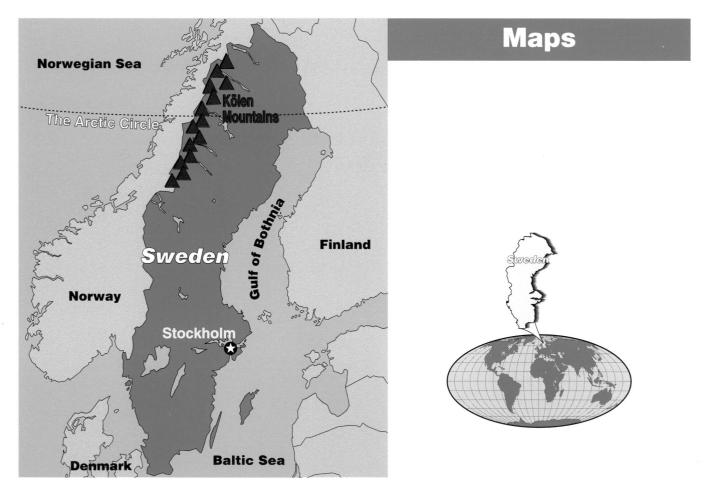

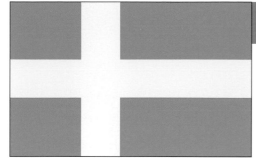

Flag

Sweden's flag is similar to the flags of the other countries in Scandinavia. This region includes Sweden, Finland, Norway, Denmark, and Iceland. The flag of each Scandinavian country has a cross on a plain background. The Swedish flag is blue with a yellow cross. Swedes began using this flag in the 1400s. They celebrate Swedish Flag Day and National Day on June 6.

Currency

The unit of currency in Sweden is the krona. One hundred öre make one krona.

In 2000, about 9 kronor equaled 1 U.S. dollar. About 6 kronor equaled 1 Canadian dollar.

The Land

Sweden is in northern Europe. The country is about as far north as Alaska. Northern Sweden lies above the Arctic Circle. Norway borders Sweden to the west and north. The Gulf of Bothnia and Finland are east of Sweden. The Baltic Sea meets Sweden's southern coast.

Sweden's landscape changes from region to region. Valleys, forests, and plains lie in the south. Sandy beaches surround bays along the coastline. The Kölen Mountains mark Sweden's western edge. Forests cover more than half of Sweden. Sweden has nearly 100,000 lakes.

Sweden is about 1,000 miles (1,600 kilometers) long from north to south. Sweden's long shape gives the country two different climates. The temperature in southern Sweden is mild. Northern Sweden is arctic. Winter temperatures there can drop to minus 40 degrees Fahrenheit (minus 40 degrees Celsius).

Sweden has snow and cold temperatures in winter.

Life at Home

Swedes live much as people in North America do. Swedes go to work or school. They like to watch TV. They go to movies, concerts, and sporting events.

In the past, most Swedes were farmers. Today, about 85 percent of Swedish people live and work in cities. Most people live in apartment buildings.

Many Swedes spend much of their time outdoors in spring and summer. They have picnics, hike in the woods, or go boating.

In most Swedish families, both parents work. The government provides day care centers for children. A national law lets one parent take 450 days off work after having a baby. Either the father or the mother takes this time off, or the parents can take turns. They still get paid during this time.

Swedes enjoy the outdoors in spring and summer.

Going to School

Swedish children must go to school for at least nine years. They start at age 6 or 7. All children study the same classes for the first six years of school. They learn math, science, social studies, art, and Swedish. Students begin to study English in the third year.

In the upper grades, students choose some of their subjects. They may take computer classes or learn about child care. Schools also offer music classes and physical education classes each week.

About 95 percent of students continue their education after primary school. They study for three years at a high school called a gymnasium.

The first two grades have a 6-hour school day. The upper grades have an 8-hour day. The school year is about nine months long. Swedish schools have breaks at Christmas, in February, and at Easter. The school year ends in June.

Swedish schools are much like those in North America.

Swedish Food

Dinners in Sweden usually include meat or fish, potatoes, vegetables, and bread. Swedes drink milk with their meals. They often drink coffee after meals.

The smörgåsbord (SMOR-gas-bord) is a Swedish tradition that began hundreds of years ago. People gathered to celebrate a wedding or a holiday. Everyone brought a dish to share. They arranged the food on a large table. Everyone helped themselves.

Swedes eat a lot of seafood, especially crayfish. Crayfish look like small lobsters. Many Swedes fish for crayfish on the first day of fishing season in August. They cook the crayfish in salt water with dill seasoning. Almost everyone holds crayfish parties. They invite their friends and put up special decorations. The crayfish are served cold with bread and cheese.

Many Swedes have crayfish parties in August.

Animals

Sweden has many forests and wilderness areas. Bears, deer, moose, rabbits, and foxes live in the forests. All these wild animals are able to survive the cold Swedish winters.

Huge herds of reindeer live in northern Sweden. The Saami people raise them for meat. The Saami are native to northern Sweden. They drink reindeer milk and use reindeer hides for clothing and tents.

The lemming is an unusual animal that lives in Sweden. These rodents are 4 to 7 inches (10 to 18 centimeters) long. In winter, their brown fur turns white. Every few years, lemmings produce so many young that their population increases quickly. They travel together in search of new places to live. Many lemmings die crossing rivers and lakes. People used to think lemmings killed themselves on purpose. Today, scientists say this is not true.

Lemmings eat grass and plants.

Sports

Swedish people have a saying, "Sport for all." They believe everyone should have the chance to take part in sports.

Sweden has long winters. Swedes take part in many winter sports. Cross-country skiing is popular. Almost every town keeps trails clear for skiers. Swedes also enjoy skating, ice hockey, ice fishing, and ice boating. Ice boaters sail on top of a frozen lake.

During summer, soccer is the most popular sport. Swedes also swim, sail, canoe, hike, and jog. Tennis also is a popular summer sport.

The Swedish government tries to help children who are good in sports. Many schools have special sports classes. Thousands of Swedes volunteer their time to coach others.

Ice skating on frozen lakes is a popular winter activity.

Saint Lucia Day

December 13 is Saint Lucia Day. Saint Lucia was a woman who lived hundreds of years ago. She gave food to the poor. Swedes remember her with special traditions.

Girls get up before dawn. The oldest girl in each family is Lucia. She wears a long white dress with a red sash around her waist. A crown of leaves with a circle of candles or electric lights tops her head. She carries a tray of coffee and buns to her parents. Her sisters dress in white and follow her. They all sing a song about Saint Lucia.

Most towns, schools, and offices choose a girl to be their official Lucia. People also elect one girl as the official Lucia for all of Sweden.

Boys sometimes join in too. Some dress as Star Boys. They wear tall hats decorated with stars and carry star-tipped wands. The children may go to hospitals, retirement homes, or other places. They sing and sometimes serve food.

Towns and offices choose a girl to represent Lucia.

This illustration shows a group of Vikings exploring new lands.

The Vikings

Today, Swedes are a peaceful people. But hundreds of years ago, some Swedes were fierce warriors called Vikings.

Vikings lived in all the Scandinavian countries. Many were farmers. But they were most famous as explorers. Vikings built special boats with shallow bottoms. They traveled all over Europe. Norwegian and Danish Vikings sailed to North America. Vikings from Sweden traveled to Russia and the Middle East.

Vikings traveled for many reasons. They traded wood, iron, furs, and other items from Sweden. They received silks, silver, and spices. They sometimes were looking for new places to live. But most of the time, Vikings attacked people in other lands. They took whatever they wanted. People in other countries were afraid of Vikings.

Hands On: Make Julgranskaramell

The julgranskaramell is a special decoration that Swedes hang on Christmas trees. The name means "Christmas tree candy."

What You Need

Empty toilet paper rolls
Treats (candy or small toys)
Brightly-colored tissue paper

Scissors
Stickers
String or ribbon

What You Do

1. Fill the toilet paper rolls with treats.
2. Wrap each roll in tissue paper with extra paper at both ends.
3. Put stickers on the edge of the tissue paper to keep it tight around the toilet paper roll.
4. Tie string or ribbon around the tissue paper at each end of the toilet paper roll.
5. Make tassels at the ends of the roll by cutting the extra paper lengthwise.
6. Exchange these gifts with your friends.

Swedes open these gifts on the julgransplundring on January 13. This name means "the plundering of the Christmas tree."

Learn to Speak Swedish

The Swedish alphabet has 29 letters. The first 26 letters are the same as English. Swedish has three extra vowels: å, ä, and ö.

boy	pojke	(POY-kyuh)
girl	flicka	(FLEE-kuh)
good-bye	hej då	(HEY DOH)
hello	hej	(HEY)
no	nej	(NEY)
thank you	tack	(TAHK)
yes	ja	(YAH)

Words to Know

arctic (ARK-tik)—very cold weather that is common in the region north of the Arctic Circle

fierce (FIHRSS)—violent or dangerous

official (uh-FISH-uhl)—approved by the people

sash (SASH)—a wide strip of material worn around the waist as a decoration

tradition (truh-DISH-uhn)—a custom, an idea, or a belief that is handed down from one generation to the next

volunteer (vol-uhn-TEEHR)—to offer to do a job without pay

warrior (WOR-ee-ur)—a soldier, or someone who is experienced in fighting battles

Read More

Carlson, Bo Kage. *Sweden.* Country Fact Files. Austin, Texas: Raintree Steck-Vaughn, 1999.

Enderlein, Cheryl L. *Christmas in Sweden.* Christmas around the World. Mankato, Minn.: Hilltop Books, 1998.

Useful Addresses and Internet Sites

Embassy of Sweden
1501 M Street NW
Washington, DC 20005

Embassy of Sweden
377 Dalhousie Street
Ottawa, ON K1N 9N8
Canada

Guide to Sweden
http://www.guidetosweden.com/index2.html
The Swedish Information Smorgasbord
http://www.sverigeturism.se/smorgasbord

Index